Adapted by Sarah Nathan

Based on the screenplay by The Wibberleys and Ted Elliott & Terry Rossio and Tim Firth

Based on a story by Hoyt Yeatman

Executive Producers Mike Stenson, Chad Oman, Duncan Henderson, David James

Produced by Jerry Bruckheimer

Directed by Hoyt Yeatman

 PRESS

NEW YORK

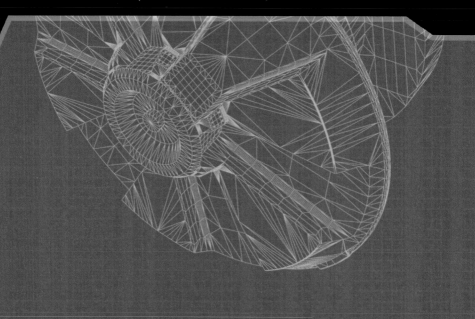

Printed in the United States of America

First Edition

1 3 5 7 9 10 8 6 4 2

Library of Congress Catalog Card Number on file

ISBN 978-1-4231-1947-0

For more Disney Press fun, visit disneybooks.com

Visit www.disney.com/g-force

CHAPTER
-1-

The G-Force was not an ordinary group of secret agents. The team was made up of three highly trained guinea pigs named Darwin, Blaster, and Juarez. Helping them was Speckles, a clever mole, and Mooch, a fly. They were on a special mission to stop a man named Leonard Saber.

Saber was one of the most successful businessmen in the world. He was also an evil mastermind being watched by the FBI. They thought he was selling military technology to bad people under the code name Project Clusterstorm. G-Force planned to stop him. But first they needed to get inside his house and download proof of his plan.

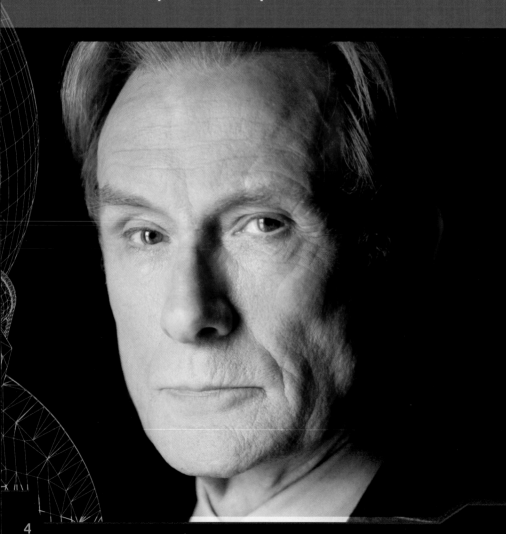

Darwin led his team inside Saber's house. Everything went well—until they were finished. A large dog was blocking Speckles's escape hole! Blaster, always ready for action, raced out to distract the dog. But he got tangled in a bush.

Luckily, Juarez, who was more cautious, was able to free him. "I won't always be here to save your furry behind," she told Blaster.

The team returned to the home of Ben Kendall, their human commander. Darwin handed over the proof of Clusterstorm. They had done it!

But when Ben went to show it to his boss, Director Killian, all they saw was a picture of a coffeemaker!

The mission was a failure. Killian shut down G-Force. But there was no way Blaster was going down without a fight.

The G-Force had no choice. They had to leave—fast! They bolted out of Ben's house using emergency capsules. "Let's do this!" Blaster shouted as he jumped into an escape capsule.

They weren't safe yet. Agents were after them! Quickly, Darwin, Blaster, Juarez, and Speckles ducked into a pet carrier to hide.

Suddenly, the box was lifted into the air. A short while later, the G-Force agents were carried into a pet store. They looked around at all the neon lights and cages. "I have never seen such fat animals in my life," Blaster observed. "Don't they have a gym around here?"

The G-Force was trapped.

CHAPTER
- 2 -

When two children named Connor and Penny walked into the pet shop with their grandfather, the animals put on their cute acts. They *had* to get adopted. It was their only hope of escape!

Hurley, a guinea pig who had been raised in a pet shop and was now a friend of the G-Force, did his best to get the children's attention. But Penny was focused on Juarez.

"I can put bows in her hair!" Penny cried.

"You try to put a bow on me, you're gonna lose a finger!" Juarez spat out. But Penny just heard squeaking, and she grinned. "She's saying she wants to come home with me!"

Juarez looked at Darwin right before she was placed in another carrier. "I know," she said. "Escape and get to Ben's house."

Before Blaster knew what was happening, he was also put in a box and handed to Connor. It looked like Juarez and Blaster were on their own.

Darwin was concerned. He didn't like it that the team was being split up. All he could do was sit tight and hope that he would be adopted next. Then he could get back to Ben's house, figure out what Project Clusterstorm really was, and rescue Juarez and Blaster.

Inside Penny's tree house, Juarez twitched in the itchy pink dress the girl had dressed her in. Then Penny put makeup *and* an earring on her! Penny smiled and admired her pet. "Don't you look pretty!"

"This is the tenth outfit!" Juarez exclaimed. She was a highly trained agent, not a fashion model!

Then Penny picked up Juarez. She placed her in front of a mirror. What Juarez saw made her scream, "I look like Paris Hilton's chihuahua!" She and Blaster *had* to get out of there.

Blaster felt a little differently. He was having a great time with Connor. Sitting in a remote-control truck, Blaster waited as Connor set up a gauntlet complete with toy soldiers, dominoes, and a long jumping ramp.

"Ready to go for the record?" Connor asked before he switched the remote control on.

Blaster grabbed the wheel and held on tight as the truck zoomed ahead. "Woo-hoo!" Blaster cried as he headed straight up a ramp.

"That was off the hook!" Blaster cheered when he landed the truck safely on the other side.

Blaster was having fun. But when Connor's mother called for him to take out the trash, Blaster knew it was his chance to save Juarez and get back to Ben's! He had the wheels—he just had to figure out how to move the truck....

Across the room, Blaster saw the remote that Connor had been using. He leaped out of the truck and scurried toward it. Blaster knew the remote was his ticket to freedom. But it was really heavy. Using all his strength, he dragged it over to the truck.

He heaved the remote inside the truck. With one hand on the steering wheel and the other on the remote, Blaster settled into a comfortable position. "I'm coming for you, Juarez!" he cried. Zipping out of the bedroom, he drove down the stairs and out the kitchen door.

While Connor was throwing out the trash, he noticed his car racing by—with Blaster at the wheel! "Hey! Come back!" he yelled. He tore off after Blaster, chasing the truck around the yard. There was no stopping Blaster, though. He raced toward the tree house—and Juarez.

In the tree house, Penny heard her brother's screams. She put Juarez in her dollhouse. "Don't go anywhere," she told the guinea pig.

"Finally." Juarez sighed. Breaking down the dollhouse door, she made her escape.

Outside, Juarez saw Blaster circling the yard.

"Juarez?" he cried. "Where are you?"

"I have to save his fur again," she said with a sigh. Then she jumped to the railing of the tree house.

CHAPTER
-4-

Juarez whistled and waved her paw to signal Blaster to turn around. Blaster was busy doing tricks and trying to get away from Connor and Penny. She gracefully flipped and landed perfectly in the seat next to Blaster.

Blaster was shocked by Juarez's appearance. She looked like a different guinea pig! "Juarez!" he exclaimed. "Why are you dressed up like that?"

Juarez gave Blaster a stern look. "One more word and I'll turn you into a small side of bacon," she warned him. Blaster innocently held up his paw. "I was gonna say hot!" he said. He shook his head and focused on his driving.

As the truck sped out of the yard, Blaster whooped with glee. He looked over at Juarez and grinned. Next destination: Ben's house. Once they were back at their headquarters, they could meet up with their leader, Darwin, and complete their mission!

By the time Blaster and Juarez reached Ben's house, they were starving. They slipped inside. There was pizza! And Darwin! He and Hurley had escaped. But poor Speckles had been left behind!

And there was more bad news! Darwin had figured out what Project Clusterstorm was—a program that would turn all of Saber's appliances into weapons! They needed to get back into Saber's mansion and destroy Clusterstorm.

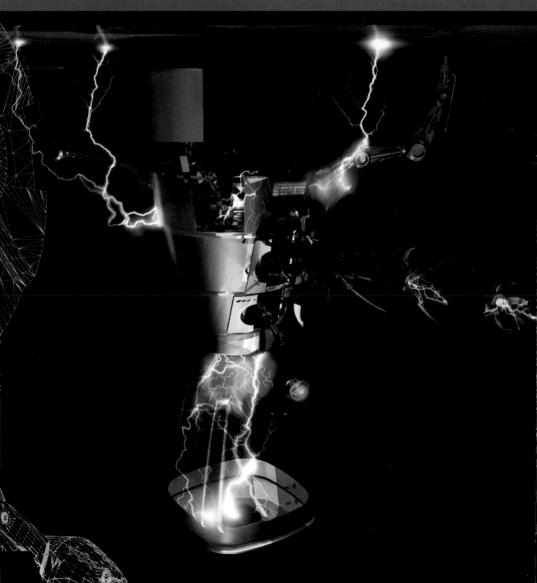

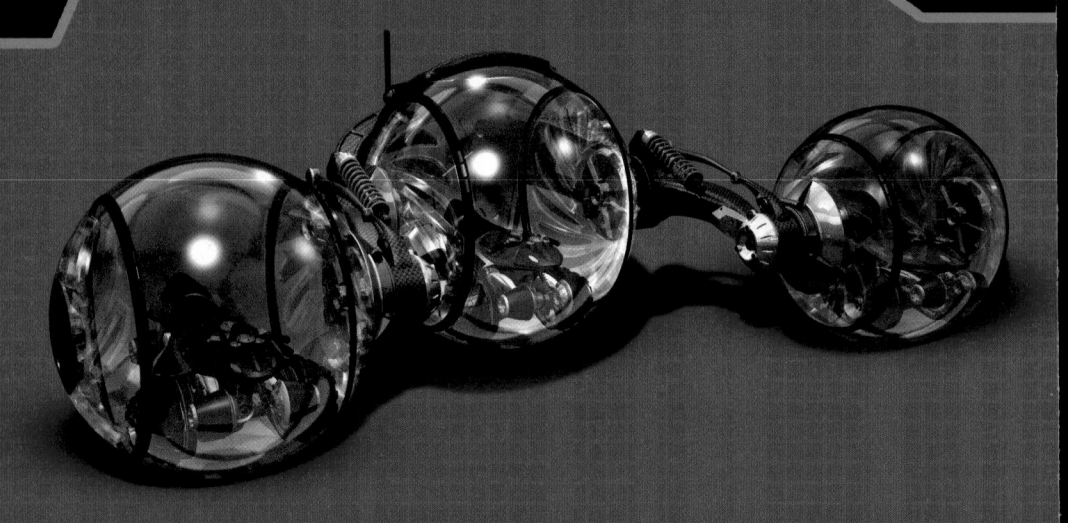

The G-Force was ready. But there was one problem. "We don't have any of our equipment," Juarez pointed out.

Ben opened a secret wall in his house to reveal fancy equipment! "Oh, man!" Blaster cried. The G-Force was back!

Ben showed Blaster a new high-tech vehicle he'd created. "Blaster, you think you can handle it?" Ben asked. Blaster raced to the front seat. "It's more like, can it handle ME? Oh, yeah, baby!"

Ben turned to Juarez and asked her to go with Blaster. "You got it," she told Ben. "This chica was built for speed!"

The rest of the G-Force geared up. Time was running out. The fate of the world was in their paws!

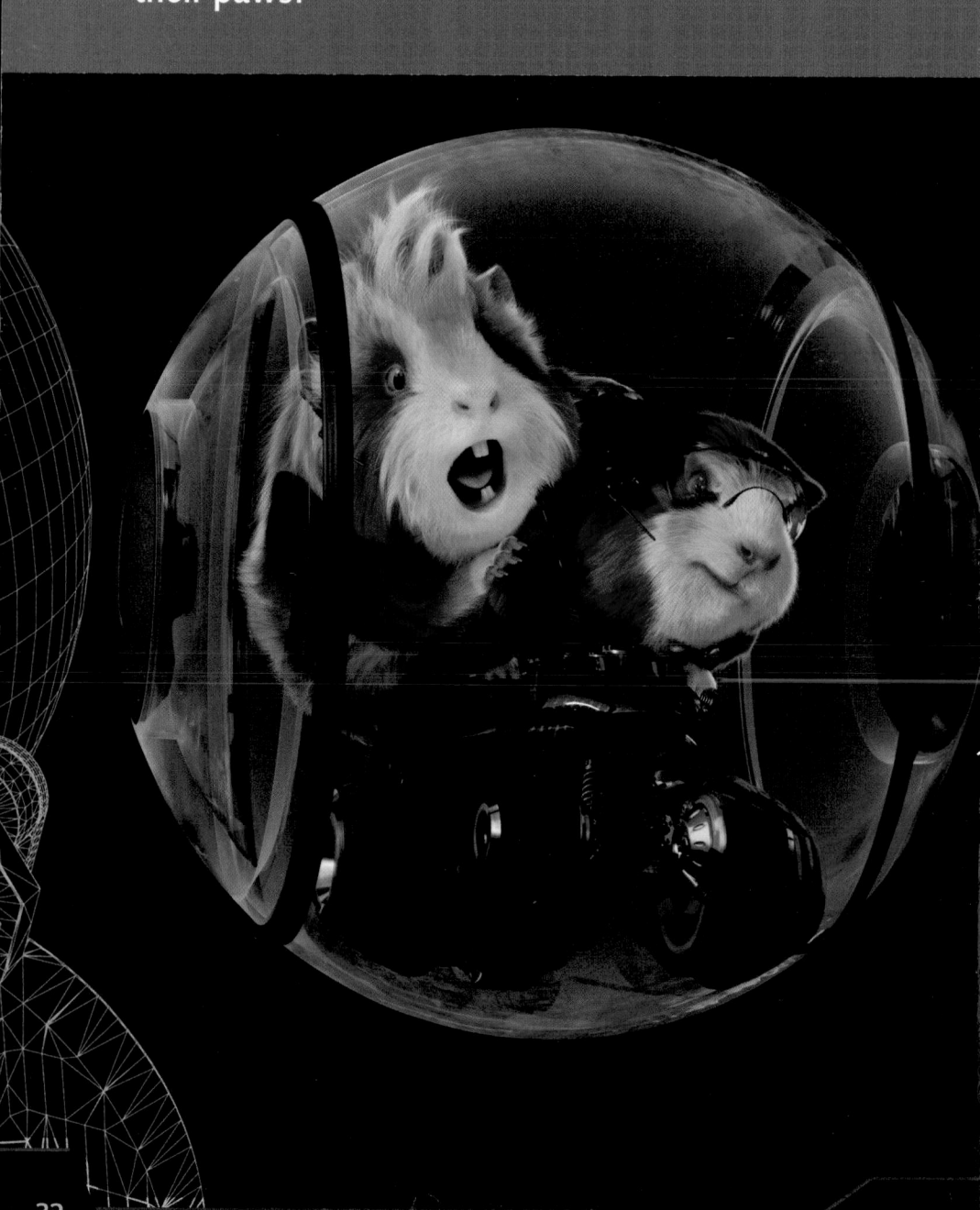

$3.99 US
Priced higher in Canada

THE POWER OF TWO . . .

Blaster and Juarez may both be part
of the G-Force, but that doesn't mean
they always get along. Blaster is too big
a show-off for Juarez's taste, and Juarez
is too uptight for Blaster's. But when
they find themselves in unfamiliar
territory without their leader, they will
have to rely on each other to escape—or
end up as house pets forever!

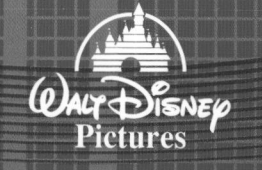

Walt **Disney**
Pictures

Disney PRESS

Visit www.disneybooks.com
Visit disney.com/g-force

ISBN 978-142311947-0

9 781423 119470